VIETNAM

The Story of a Marine

Dee Phillips

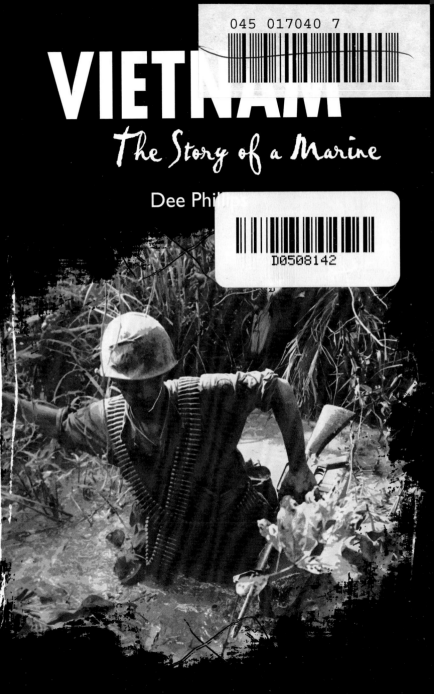

READZONE

READZONE

First published in this edition 2014

British Library Cataloguing in Publication Data (CIP) is available for this title.

ISBN 978-1-78322-513-2

Printed in Malta by Melita Press

Developed and Created by Ruby Tuesday Books Ltd
Project Director – Ruth Owen
Designer – Elaine Wilkinson

Images courtesy of Alamy (pages 16–17c), AP/Press Association Images (page 24), Corbis (pages 1, 13t, 15t, 26t, 28, 30, 38–39, 43, 44b), Getty Images (page 23) and Shutterstock.

Acknowledgements
With thanks to Lorraine Petersen, Educational Consultant, for her help in the development and creation of these books

Visit our website: www.readzonebooks.com

Every day we went on patrol.

The Viet Cong were everywhere.

Hiding in the jungles. Hiding in villages.

We had to find them, before they found us.

VIETNAM
The Story of a Marine

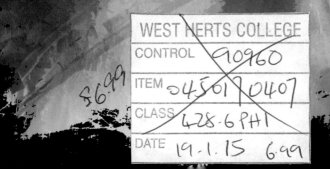

In the 1960s, South Vietnam was at war.

Their enemies were North Vietnam and an army of rebels from the South called the Viet Cong.

The United States supported the government of South Vietnam.

American troops were sent to Vietnam
to fight.

Some young Americans enlisted.
They knew they might go to Vietnam.

Others did not have a choice.
They were made to join the armed forces
by the US government. This was known
as the draft.

Many Americans did not want their
country to fight in this faraway war.

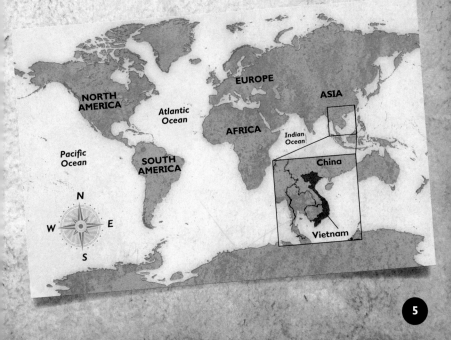

I look into her eyes.
She looks into mine.
She's just a kid. Maybe 15 or 16.
Her rifle is just inches from my face.

She screams at me.
I don't know what she's saying.
I only know one thing.
I don't want to die in Vietnam.

I look into the girl's eyes.
She jabs her rifle at my face.

No more than a second passes,
but time stands still.
I hear Eddie's voice.

*"You won't be around to hear
Mom's screams."*

Eddie. My brother. My twin.
Mom always said she could
feel us fighting inside her.
We came into the world on
the same day.

That was the last time we ever
agreed on anything.

I couldn't wait for high
school to be over.
All I ever wanted was to
be a marine.
There was a war going on
and I wanted in!

I signed up as soon as I was 18.

All Eddie ever wanted was
to be a doctor.
Eddie didn't agree with killing.
He didn't think Americans should
fight in someone else's war.

"Don't you see the bodies on
the news?" he shouted.
"You won't be here when they
knock on the door."

"You won't be around to hear
Mom's screams."

NOT OUR SONS
NOT YOUR SONS
NOT THEIR SONS

I couldn't wait to get to boot camp.
I got off the bus feeling like a man.
By the end of my first day, I was a
scared kid.
A scared kid with a shaved head.

RUNNING

POLISHING

SHOOTING

MARCHING

PRESS-UPS

SIT-UPS

SCRUBBING

If one guy screwed up, we all got punished.
I wished Eddie was there with me.

The scared kid turned into a marine.
I went home on leave.
Mom cried when she saw me in
my uniform.
But Eddie couldn't look me in the eye.

"I can't believe you're going to fight this
war!" he shouted.
"Well, I'm proud to fight for my country,"
I shouted back. "You're just a coward!"

It was the worst fight we
ever had.

The girl soldier jabs her rifle at my face.
She screams at me.
I don't know what she's saying.
I only know one thing.
I'm going to have to shoot this girl.
It's her or me.

I couldn't wait to get to Vietnam.
Every day we went on patrol.
There were no battlefields in this war.
The Viet Cong were everywhere.
Hiding in the jungles.
Hiding in villages.

We had to find them, before they
found us.

You think you know what fear is.
But you don't.
We were on patrol in rice fields.
We came under fire.
I crawled through the water on my belly.
Bullets hit the water all around me.

Our choppers flew in.
They blew the enemy apart and
rescued us.
That was a good day.

You think you can imagine what death
looks like.
But you can't.

We were on patrol in a jungle.

One of our guys touched a trip wire.
The landmine blew him apart.

I found his dog tags hanging from a tree.

I missed my brother.
Every time I smoked with the guys,
I thought of Eddie.
Every time I heard a joke, I wanted to
tell him.

I thought about the fight.

We'd patch it up when I got home.

The months passed by.
Some days were boring.
Some days were terrifying.
But I loved being a marine.
I was proud to fight for my country.

But it was tough.
I lost so many friends.

Then came that night.
We were searching a village.
There were Viet Cong
hiding there.
I crept into a hut.
That's where I found the girl.

She jabs her rifle at my face.

She screams at me.

I'm going to have to shoot
this girl.

It's her or me.

BANG!

I wake up with a jolt.
I lie in the darkness.
I didn't die that night, but I relive it
in my dreams.

Again and again for nearly 50 years.

Somehow I survived that night.
A Viet Cong shell hit the hut.
It blew the young girl apart.
I crawled from the hut, burned but alive.

Somehow I survived that war.

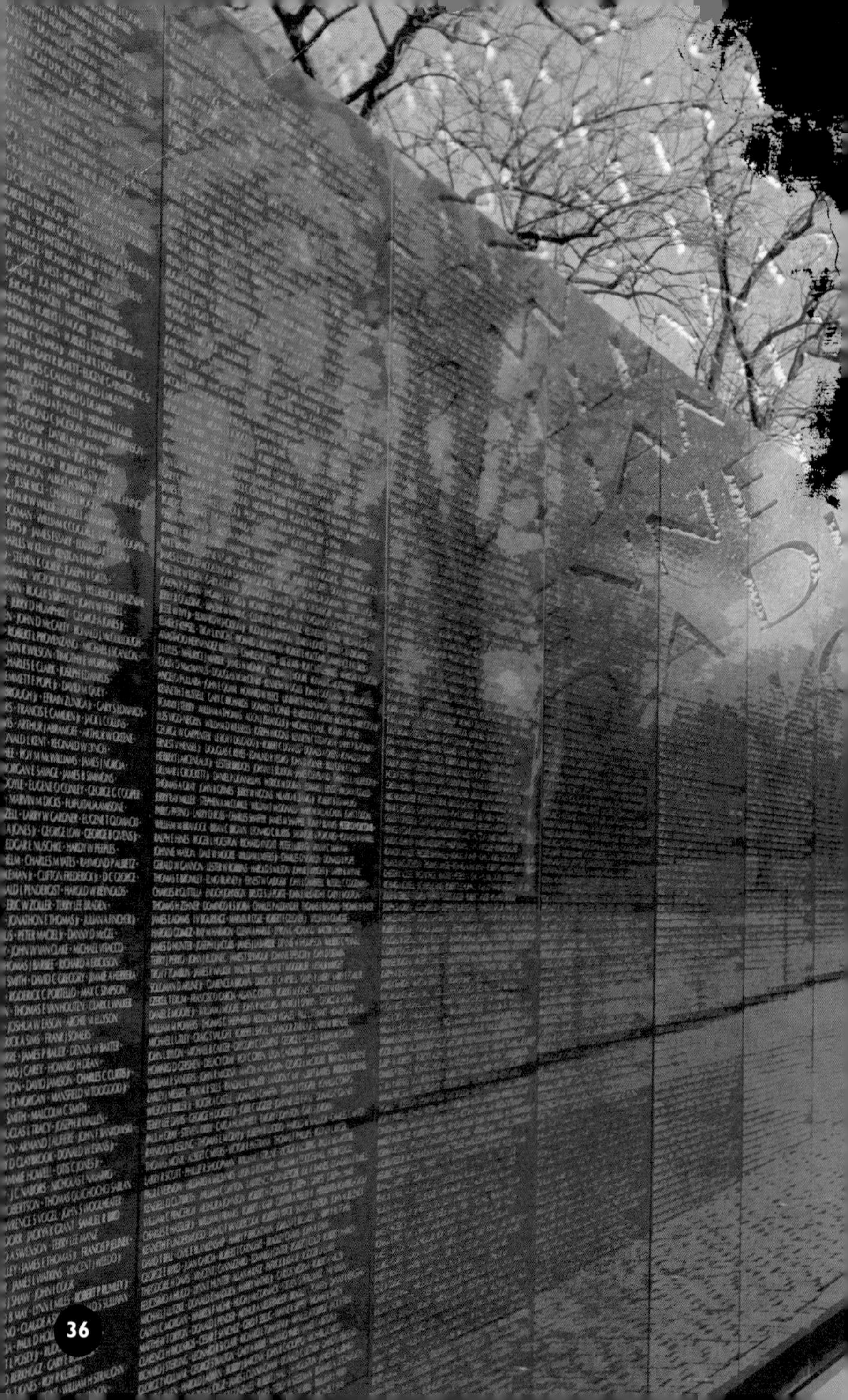

Now I come to The Wall every year.
I look at the thousands of names.
The names of the guys who never
came home.

I slowly walk along the wall.
After all these years, I know where
I'm heading.

In the end, even Eddie had to go.
He was drafted and sent to Vietnam.
Eddie. My brother. The coward.
I couldn't have been more wrong.

Eddie was killed in Vietnam.
He took a bullet to the head.
There was a little kid.
She was trapped between our
guys and the enemy.
Eddie died trying to save that
little kid.

He was right about one thing.
I wasn't around to hear Mom's screams.

I find his name on the wall.
Eddie. My brother. My twin.
We never did patch up that fight.

I gently touch the cool stone and
close my eyes.
I just hope that he's out there
somewhere.

And that he knows....

Vietnam: *Behind the Story*

In the 1960s, North Vietnam was a communist nation. The government controlled land, business and property. People were not as free to make changes to their lives as people living in a democratic nation, such as the United States. South Vietnam was not communist. North Vietnam was at war with South Vietnam. The North also supported the Viet Cong, an army of communist rebels in the South.

So why did the US get involved in the Vietnam War? The US claimed that if South Vietnam fell, it would lead to communism spreading to other parts of the world. The US became an ally, or partner, of South Vietnam.

Many Americans opposed the war. They did not believe that fighting in Vietnam protected democracy. They did not trust the South Vietnamese government. A large anti-war movement grew up.

In 1973, the US withdrew from Vietnam. In 1975, North Vietnam took over all of Vietnam. Many Americans felt the war was a terrible waste of lives. More than 58,000 Americans died in Vietnam. It's estimated that more than 3 million Vietnamese soldiers and civilians were killed.

The Draft

During the 1960s and 1970s, young American men had to be available to serve in the military. When the US entered the Vietnam War, many of them were called up, or drafted. They had to join the US armed forces, even if they didn't agree with the war and didn't want to fight.

Thousands of Americans protested against the war at meetings and marches.

END THE
WAR
IN VIETNAM
NOW

Vietnam – What's next?

I JUST HOPE THAT HE KNOWS

ON YOUR OWN

At the end of the story, the main character thinks about his brother, Eddie. He has lots of feelings that he would like Eddie to know about. Look back through the story.

- What clues to the brothers' relationship and feelings can you find?

- What things do you think the marine would like to tell Eddie if he could?

IN BLACK AND WHITE

ON YOUR OWN

During wars, photographers and film makers often put themselves in danger to record what is happening. Many photos from the Vietnam War are famous because they had a powerful effect on people back home.

The photos in this book that show soldiers in Vietnam are real photos from the war. Which one do you think is the most powerful? How does the photo make you feel?

WAR SONGS

Many songs were written about the Vietnam War. You can find them and listen to them online. Then try writing your own song about the war. You can use the story of the twin brothers as your inspiration or think of a different idea for the theme of your Vietnam War song.

THE WALL

The twin brothers are characters in a story. The things they experienced in Vietnam happened to thousands of young men, though. At the end of the book, the marine visits the Vietnam Veterans Memorial (The Wall) in Washington D.C. in the United States.

Find out more about The Wall, the war and the ways in which the people who died in Vietnam are remembered, by visiting:

http://www.vvmf.org/

45

Titles in the
Yesterday's Voices
series

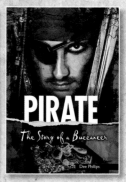

We jump from our ship and attack. But something feels wrong. I know this place….

We face each other. Two proud samurai. Revenge burns in my heart.

We saw a treasure ship. Up went our black flag. They could not escape….

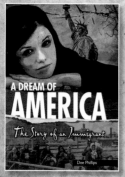

The work is so hard. I miss my home. Will my dream of America come true?

I jumped from the plane. I carried fake papers, a gun and a radio. Now I was Sylvie, a resistance fighter….

Every day we went on patrol. The Viet Cong hid in jungles and villages. We had to find them, before they found us.

GLADIATOR

The Story of a Fighter

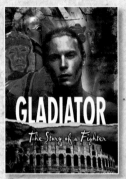

RUNAWAY

The Story of a Slave

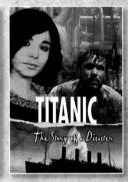

TITANIC

The Story of a Disaster

I waited deep below the arena. Then it was my turn to fight. Kill or be killed!

I cannot live as a slave any longer. Tonight, I will escape and never go back.

The ship is sinking into the icy sea. I don't want to die. Someone help us!

OVER THE TOP

The Story of a Soldier

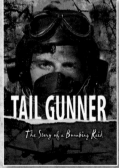

TAIL GUNNER

The Story of a Bombing Raid

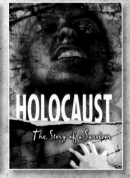

HOLOCAUST

The Story of a Survivor

I'm waiting in the trench. I am so afraid. Tomorrow we go over the top.

Another night. Another bombing raid. Will this night be the one when we don't make it back?

They took my clothes and shaved my head. I was no longer a human.